I0600442

Break of Day

A Play

Stephen Fife

A SAMUEL FRENCH ACTING EDITION

FOUNDED 1830

SAMUELFRENCH.COM
SAMUELFRENCH-LONDON.CO.UK

MUSIC USE NOTE

Licensees are solely responsible for obtaining formal written permission from copyright owners to use copyrighted music in the performance of this play and are strongly cautioned to do so. If no such permission is obtained by the licensee, then the licensee must use only original music that the licensee owns and controls. Licensees are solely responsible and liable for all music clearances and shall indemnify the copyright owners of the play(s) and their licensing agent, Samuel French, against any costs, expenses, losses and liabilities arising from the use of music by licensees. Please contact the appropriate music licensing authority in your territory for the rights to any incidental music.

IMPORTANT BILLING AND CREDIT REQUIREMENTS

If you have obtained performance rights to this title, please refer to your licensing agreement for important billing and credit requirements.

BREAK OF DAY was first produced by Francesca Rollins at the Lillian Theater in Hollywood, CA on October 7, 1999. The Production ran for 40 performances, closing on December 12, 1999. The cast and crew were as follows:

VINCENT	Brendan Ford
PASTOR THEODORUS	Victor Raider-Wexler
THEO	Brian Gaskill
KAY VOS	Leslie Hunt
ANNA	Kathleen Bunny Gibson
SIEN, MAID, MINER'S WIFE	Ali Burns
MAGDA, MINER'S WIFE	Meredith Morton

Casting Note: Through the Hollywood run, Ali Burns stepped in for Meredith Morton and played **MAGDA** and **MINER'S WIFE** (in addition to **SIEN, MAID,** and **MINER'S WIFE**) during the second half of the show.

DIRECTOR	Billy Hayes
PRODUCER	Francesca Rollins
ASSOCIATE PRODUCERS	Jon Sweet, Robert Amico, Gary Blumsack
CASTING DIRECTOR	Zora Dehorter
SET DESIGNER	Scott Seidman
LIGHTING DESIGNER	Dana Kilgore
COSTUME DESIGNER	Jeanine Payton
SOUND DESIGNER	Peter Stenshoel
STAGE MANAGER	H.P. Drake III
ASSOCIATE PRODUCERS	Jon Sweet, Robert Amico, Gary Blumsack
SOUND OPERATOR	Trudi Cohen
SET CONSTRUCTION	Neil Wilson, Dusty Engelbrecht
PUBLICITY	R.S. Bailey
HOUSE MANAGER	Jeanette Cosack
PRODUCTION PHOTOGRAPHERS	Terry Israel, Geoff Seaton

Time: 1880 to 1885

Place: The presbytery house in Zundert, Northern Holland, and its environs. Also, one scene in a run-down boardinghouse in Amsterdam.

CHARACTERS

VINCENT VAN GOGH – Male, 30-35

THEO VAN GOGH – Male, 25-32

THOMAS (Coalminer), **REVEREND PETERSON** – Male, 35-45 (These characters could be played by someone who also has other associations with the production – such as Assistant Stage Manager.)

PASTOR THEODORUS VAN GOG – Male, 58-65

ANNA VAN GOGH, **MINING WOMAN** – Female, 52-57(This character appears only in the second scene.)

KAY VOS, **MINER'S WIFE** – Female, 30-35 (This character appears only in the second scene.)

MAGDA, **MINER'S WIFE**, **MAID**, **SIEN KELLER** – Female, 25-30 (These roles can also be divided up between two actresses.)

SETTING & TIME

The play takes place between 1880 – 1885, mostly in a small town in Northern Holland. A variety of settings are required, most of them centered around the parsonage of Pastor Theodorus van Gogh. A few short scenes takes place in the mining town of the Borinage, Belgium and two others take place in Amsterdam.

PRODUCTION NOTES

SCENE DESIGN

Minimal settings to suggest locations. A palette of grays, blacks, off-whites, browns, and occasional reds. A scrim or screen is needed, on which to rear-project a slide of van Gogh's "The Potato Eaters"–unless another way is found to dramatize this image. In the premiere production, the set designer used two rear-projector screens to project slides of paintings (some by van Gogh, most not) which he had digitally altered to convey both a sense of place and a mood.

SCRIPT HISTORY

Previous versions received readings at Primary Stages Co. (NYC), Shenandoah Playwrights Retreat in Virginia, and Nexus Ensemble in LA under the title "Light and Darkness." An earlier version of "Break of Day" premiered at the Lillian Theatre, Hollywood, on 10/1/99, directed by Billy Hayes, produced by Francesca Rollins. Big thanks to Billy. The current version has been extensively reconceived and rewritten since that production.

AUTHOR'S NOTE

I was drawn to this story by Vincent's Letters, with their unsurpassed sense of intimacy, and the mythic scope they present of a modern religious journey. All the events in the play are taken from descriptions in Vincent's Letters or from secondary source material. There are mysteries and paradoxes at the core of Vincent's work and life that can never really be captured, but which I've done my best to dramatize.

"At break of day I seek a path to a world unknown."

– from a Noh Play by Zenchiku

For Billy, a great director and a better friend.
And for my darling daughter,
who burst onto the scene during rehearsals.

ACT I

Scene One

(Lights up on an unfinished version of **VINCENT***'s painting "The Potato Eaters," which has been rear-projected on a screen; a blank swath cuts across the middle: instead of a family at supper, we see only two figures, one at each end of the table, with a huge gap in-between. Then the light widens out, revealing* **VINCENT***, 32, standing in front of the unfinished painting, wearing an old soldier's tunic, workman's pants and old shoes, everything splattered with paint. He faces* **MAGDA***, 25, a peasant girl dressed in traditional Dutch garb. It is May, 1885.)*

VINCENT. Oh God…

MAGDA. I am terribly sorry, Herr Vincent.

VINCENT. How will I… How will I ever complete this now?

MAGDA. You have bigger things to worry about, sir. Just forget about your painting.

VINCENT. Never.

*(***VINCENT** *suddenly grabs her by the shoulders, shakes her, brings his arm back to slap her…then drops his hand, turning away.)*

What am I going to do?

MAGDA. I really didn't mean for this to happen, Herr Vincent.

VINCENT. Leave, Magda.

MAGDA. You have to believe me, sir. When they asked me those questions, I –

VINCENT. Just go away.

MAGDA. I was only being honest, Herr Vincent. You wouldn't want me to lie, would you?

VINCENT. Now!

MAGDA. I'll pray for you, Vincent. I will.

(There is a slight smile on her face as she exits.)

VINCENT. How did this happen? How could this ever happen?

(He looks back at the painting for a long beat.)

I will find you, do you hear me? I have not come all this way just to leave your face blank. I will figure you out. I will paint you.

*(***VINCENT*** turns and exits. The painting fades from the screen.)*

Scene Two

(Five years earlier: The stage is suddenly lit by glaring electric light. Dust-smeared coalminers and bundled women with swaddled babies trudge across the stage. There is an Offstage clanging and shouting, a chaotic, exhausted, end-of-the-world feeling to it all. **THEO** *wanders on, very lost. He is 25, well-dressed, a Parisian businessman.)*

THEO. Excuse me? I'm looking for the preacher –

(The miner makes an obscene gesture, goes off.)

(takes out his wallet) I'm trying to locate the preacher here. If you can help me find him, then –

(A young woman with a baby is about to reach for the money, when she sees a second woman watching her. The young woman backs away. **THEO** *holds out the money to her.)*

Look, you can have the money… I'm trying to find Preacher Vincent… I've come a long way.

(Ominous silence. **THEO** *shrugs, pockets his money, tips his hat, exits. The women disperse, as the lighting changes to a smoky firelight.* **VINCENT**, *27, climbs out of a dark pit, covered all over with coat dust. He seems like a shadow figure. He looks over the devastated landscape around him, picks up sketchpad, working with hard furious strokes. Lights go down on this scene.)*

Scene Three

(Lights rise on a **PASTOR***'s study in the van Gogh parsonage, Northern Holland, 1881.* **PASTOR THEODORUS VAN GOGH***, 58, sits at his writing table. The room is filled with midday sunlight.* **ANNA VAN GOGH***, 54, enters, carrying a tea service & plate of biscuits.)*

ANNA. Theodorus?

PASTOR THEO. *(working on a sermon)* Yes, dear? *(looks up)* Oh.

*(***PASTOR** *moves a book aside;* **ANNA** *puts down the tray.)*

ANNA. *(pours tea)* Theo's outside. He wants to speak with you first. I'm convinced that things weren't as bad as Reverend Pietersen said.

PASTOR THEO. *(takes out a printed handbill)* Have you seen this? The sexton over at St. Mary's extends his sympathy for "your eldest son's recent misfortunes."

ANNA. *(looks at handbill)* I don't see what's so bad...

PASTOR THEO. Read it.

ANNA. I've read it already.

PASTOR THEO. Out loud.

ANNA. "We at St. Mary's Parish would like to extend our deepest sympathies to the good Pastor Theodorus van Gogh of the Dutch Lutheran Church for his eldest son's recent misfortunes. Just as all of us – regardless of denomination – rejoiced when Vincent won his assignment as Evangelical minister to the mining camps in Belgium, so now we feel great sadness at the news" –

PASTOR THEO. I'm sure he toasted it with a glass of good Catholic wine.

ANNA. Theodorus...

PASTOR THEO. It reflects on all of us, Anna.

ANNA. I don't want you to say a word of this. Just try to make him feel at home.

(**PASTOR** *nods, sips his tea.* **ANNA** *exits.* **THEO** *enters.*)

PASTOR THEO. So, boy: give me the toll of the latest disaster.

THEO. Father, there's no need to start out –

PASTOR THEO. Don't try to spare my feelings, boy. Tell me the worst.

THEO. I don't think it's in anyone's interest to –

PASTOR THEO. Don't mince words with me, boy. I have to hear it.

THEO. Vincent has been through a lot. He needs our love and support.

PASTOR THEO. *(nods)* Look, you want to put the best face on a bad situation. He's my son, so I'll have to bear with it, but –

THEO. No. Vincent has something so unusual.

PASTOR THEO. Well, now we finally agree.

THEO. I really saw it for the first time when I went to the mining camp.

PASTOR THEO. You mean, in his artwork?

THEO. Well – yes. In a way.

PASTOR THEO. So you're honestly telling me that his artwork is good?

THEO. Well, the sketches were bad, I admit it. Very crude. But there was something else.

PASTOR THEO. Maybe what you saw was your love for your brother.

THEO. *(shakes his head)* His work made me understand, in a way I never had before, that there is a God.

PASTOR THEO. In a way you never had before?

THEO. I mean, I've felt it in your sermons, of course. But I'm talking about something I've rarely experienced, outside of Millet...

PASTOR THEO. Really, Theo. You see God in a bad sketch? That's not like you. *(***THEO** *shrugs.*)*
And you're willing to provide support for him?

THEO. We all have to do what we can to help him.

PASTOR THEO. That goes without saying. Now send him in.

THEO. I'd like to be here too.

PASTOR THEO. Why?

THEO. Vincent is still in a fragile condition.

PASTOR THEO. I will see him alone.

THEO. I really wish you'd reconsider – *(moves toward the door)* Just please try to be gentle –

> *(PASTOR THEO glares at him. THEO exits. Pause. VINCENT enters, wearing a gray suit; stands awkwardly.)*

PASTOR THEO. Sit down, boy. *(VINCENT sits.)* Tea?

VINCENT. No thank you.

PASTOR THEO. Have a biscuit.

> *(VINCENT declines, PASTOR takes one.)*

So: how do you like being back? It's almost like you never left, isn't it? *(pause)*

You're my eldest son, boy, and if anything was to happen to me, I hope you'd be able to... That is, we all have our responsibilities, both in this family and in the world, and it's my greatest wish, boy, that someday you'll have your own –

VINCENT. *(takes a biscuit)* Oh yes, me too. I think children are the greatest gift. I will give you grandchildren, I promise.

PASTOR THEO. Of course your mother and I would be so happy if –

VINCENT. If I had a choice between making art and making children, I would make children. Lots of them.

PASTOR THEO. But you need money first.

VINCENT. So right now I'll work on my painting.

PASTOR THEO. If you think that will make money...

VINCENT. Oh, I'm sure it will.

PASTOR THEO. *(sips tea)* Is there anything you'd like to tell me about what happened in the mining camps? *(pause)* We heard some terrible stories from Reverend Pietersen.

VINCENT. I had my job to do, and I did it the best that I could. Reverend Pietersen had his job to do, and he did it.

PASTOR THEO. Reverend Pietersen was there representing the church.

VINCENT. So was I.

PASTOR THEO. Well, I hardly think you can compare –

(**VINCENT** *picks up the biscuit, holds onto it.*)

You were there for a trial period, boy, you had to show the authorities they could trust you –

(**VINCENT** *puts the biscuit in his pocket.*)

I know it's not always easy, boy, knowing the right thing to do.

VINCENT. You don't seem to have any problem.

PASTOR THEO. Oh, that's not true, believe me. But I find that if I put my trust in the Lord, He doesn't –

(**VINCENT** *fidgets, nervous, bored. Pause:* **PASTOR** *pours himself more tea.*)

I think we should have a clear understanding of what the rules will be while you're here.

VINCENT. The rules?

PASTOR THEO. That's right. There are rules wherever you go in the world, and this is no exception.

VINCENT. I don't see the need for them.

PASTOR THEO. No?

VINCENT. If you respect my rights and I respect yours, then there will be no problems.

PASTOR THEO. And what are your rights?

VINCENT. Simply to be left alone in my studio to do my own work.

PASTOR THEO. I'm afraid it's not that simple... *(He takes out the handbill, hands it to* **VINCENT.***)*
In case you've forgotten, we have twice as many Protestants as Catholics in this village, and the sexton will stop at nothing.

VINCENT. *(hands back the handbill)* It's none of his business.

PASTOR THEO. We have had incidents here. Name-calling. Stone-throwing. And two Catholic boys toppled over some graves in our cemetery.

VINCENT. You caught these boys?

PASTOR THEO. Why?

VINCENT. Because I'd like to speak with them.

PASTOR THEO. That's not the point.

VINCENT. Someone needs to speak with them.

PASTOR THEO. Do you plan to be in regular attendance at Church while you're here?

VINCENT. I haven't given it much thought...

PASTOR THEO. Do you plan to show up at all?

VINCENT. I don't know.

PASTOR THEO. I'm telling you right now that I expect you to be in church on a regular basis.

VINCENT. But if I no longer feel any –

PASTOR THEO. I don't care what you feel. That's between you and Your Maker.

VINCENT. Exactly.

PASTOR THEO. But as long as you're living under my roof, I will not have any behavior that undercuts me. Is that understood? That means no eccentricities, boy, and showing up at church with the other. Do you think you can do that?

VINCENT. But Theo said that you understood my –

PASTOR THEO. I don't care what Theo said. Do you hear me?

VINCENT. *(He stands.)* I would really like to speak with those two boys.

PASTOR THEO. They have already been admonished and sent on their way.

VINCENT. I would still be willing to –

PASTOR THEO. The church has a limited scope. It cannot do everything. That's where you went wrong in that mining town.

VINCENT. Really? And I thought you'd be proud of me.

PASTOR THEO. Why?

VINCENT. I thought I was doing what you would have wanted me to.

(VINCENT moves upstage right, to where THEO stands near an acacia tree and rock. Transition: VINCENT's memory-tinged vision of the coalmines: the stage is suddenly lit by the glaring electric light. A coal-smeared miner comforts a young mother with a swaddled baby. Offstage there is again that clanging and shouting.)

THEO. Vincent? Vincent?

(Lights fade on the miner, etc., sounds diminish. Lights up fully on THEO and the acacia tree.)

Are you alright?

VINCENT. It's hard to believe that I'm back in our clearing… It feels like a dream.

THEO. Well, you are back. And it's a good thing.

VINCENT. Is it? I don't want to bring father and mother any more pain.

THEO. They love you, Vincent. They just want you to be happy.

VINCENT. Look Theo… Whatever I do – it's your work as much as it's mine.

THEO. Just remember, you've come back here to stay.

VINCENT. I don't know the future.

THEO. Well, I do. You'll be here until you're good enough to join me in Paris. Isn't that what I'm sending you money for?

VINCENT. So this is about money?

THEO. That's right. That's all I care about.

VINCENT. You'll get your money's worth.

THEO. Oh? What security can you give me?

VINCENT. There is no security.

THEO. That's not very reassuring. *(pause)* I have to leave for that train soon…

VINCENT. We will show them, boy. We will show them.

*(**VINCENT** clasps **THEO** 's hand, gives it a strong shake. Lights up also on **PASTOR** at pulpit downstage left, while remaining on **VINCENT** and **THEO**, as **THEO** bids **VIN** goodbye, exits.)*

PASTOR THEO. *(speaks to audience as "Congregation," ending a sermon)* As many of you know, my eldest son recently returned to us after spending a time doing God's work in the coalmines…

*(**VINCENT** exits. Lights down on the clearing.)*

He has now decided to show his love of the Lord through his artwork…so if you meet up with him in the fields… I hope you will say hello and make him feel welcome… For our part, we are glad, very glad, to have him back. No matter what anyone else might have you think…

*(Lights fade on Preacher, rise on the van Goghs' diningroom, where **ANNA** is preparing the table for supper, as **VINCENT** sits sketching her. The spread of food should resemble a scene from a Dutch still life: Large bowl in the center, loaf of fresh-baked bread with a knife to slice it, dish of butter. Also, the remnants of a ham & a quarter-wheel of cheese. **ANNA** seems happy to have **VINCENT** here, but uncomfortable being watched.)*

ANNA. *(wipes her hands on her apron)* You're not going to be unlucky anymore, do you hear?

VINCENT. *(sketching)* I don't believe in luck.

ANNA. That's because you've never had any.

VINCENT. We all do the best we can, don't we?

ANNA. I hope you'll remember that with your father. We all need to be more forgiving.

(**PASTOR THEO** *joins them.* **VINCENT** *puts down his sketchpad.* **ANNA** *removes her apron, sits. All bow their heads in prayer.*)

PASTOR THEO. Give us grateful hearts, our Father, and make us mindful of the needs of others, through Jesus Christ, our Lord. Amen.

ANNA. Amen.

VINCENT. Amen.

(**ANNA** *stands, serving the soup.*)

PASTOR THEO. *(gets his bowl from* **ANNA***)* That looks very good.

ANNA. *(serving* **VINCENT***)* Thank you.

PASTOR THEO. It smells very good too.

ANNA. *(serves herself)* It's only my old pea soup, dear. Nothing special.

PASTOR THEO. Shouldn't we give thanks for those things we have, no matter how familiar they are?

VINCENT. Of course, father.

ANNA. *(to* **PASTOR***)* Some bread, dear?

PASTOR THEO. That's allright, I'll do it. *(He stands, slices bread.)* A slice of bread, Vincent?

(**VINCENT** *nods.* **PASTOR** *slices another piece, hands cutting board to* **VIN.***)*

ANNA. *(to* **VIN***)* We're going to be friends again, aren't we?

VINCENT. Of course we are, mother.

PASTOR THEO. *(Stands, carves the ham. To* **ANNA***:)* Have you told him about Kay yet?

ANNA. No dear. I thought we would both tell him later.

VINCENT. What about Cousin Kay? Is she getting married again?

PASTOR THEO. The idea!

VINCENT. Why not?

PASTOR THEO. Pastor Vos is still warm in his grave.

ANNA. Theodorus!

VINCENT. What does that matter? I never felt they were right for each other.

PASTOR THEO. Now that's exactly the kind of thing you mustn't say when she comes here.

ANNA. What your father means is –

PASTOR THEO. Reverend Stricker is counting on us to help her get over her grief. I know the two of you were good friends in Amsterdam, and she's looking forward to seeing you… *(slicing cheese)*

ANNA. She said so herself in her letter.

PASTOR THEO. But we have to be careful. She's in a very delicate state, and we mustn't say anything to upset her. So I'm counting on you to help.

VINCENT. I understand.

PASTOR THEO. Good. *(He sits.)* I want to make sure she takes a good report back to Stricker.

ANNA. Of course she will, Theodorus. Why shouldn't she? *(pause)*

(Lights fade on diningroom. **VINCENT** *stands, picks up sketchpad, turns upstage: Once again the stage is lit by the glaring electric light. A coal-smeared miner breaks up rocks with a pick. Offstage there is still that clanging and shouting.* **KAY VOS***, 33, a pensive woman in black, enters, stands by the acacia tree.)*

KAY. *(calls)* Vincent? Vincent? *(Clanging stops. Light dims to half-level on miner.)*

*(***VINCENT*** enters the clearing, working on a sketch.)*

It's so beautiful out here.

VINCENT. Yes.

KAY. What you said before was quite right, it's really a shame to live in the city when there are places like this… It must make you feel very close to God.

*(***VINCENT*** nods.)*

And you're doing so well.

VINCENT. You think so?

KAY. You're really getting better and better. Let's see what you've done.

(**VINCENT** *gives her the sketchbook.* **KAY** *looks it over.*)

I almost envy you.

VINCENT. Why?

KAY. You have something which makes you feel so alive. So important.

VINCENT. So do you, Kay.

KAY. *(pause)* Oh yes, I'd feel really lost now if not for my son.

VINCENT. You're still young. You'll marry again.

KAY. No.

VINCENT. That sounds so final. (**VIN** *takes the sketchbook from* **KAY**, *re-works the sketch.*)

KAY. Don't feel you have to stay. It's so peaceful… *(pause)* Friedrich was a very good man, but he didn't have much patience. It surprised me a bit. I guess my father set an example…

VINCENT. I always felt he got a little caught up in things…

KAY. That was Friedrich.

VINCENT. I didn't think he was good enough for you.

KAY. What makes you say that?

(**VINCENT** *walks off, working.*)

Friedrich always liked you. He was always sticking up for you to my father.

VINCENT. Impossible!

(*He throws down the sketch. Lights up to three-quarter level. On the coalmining scene: A coalminer –* **THOMAS** *– is working.*)

THOMAS. *(coalminer)* We miss you in church, Monsieur Preacher. You brought people back. You made them see God again. Now they are leaving.

KAY. Vincent… *(picks up pad, holds it out to* **VINCENT***)*

THOMAS. I am glad to help Monsieur Vincent with your artwork.

KAY. *(still holding pad)* You must have more patience, Vincent. It takes time.

VINCENT. *(turns)* What? Oh. I don't have it.

KAY. What do you mean?

VINCENT. I've already wasted so much...

KAY. You've just started.

THOMAS. Will God be there too, Monsieur Vincent? I mean, in your artwork?

KAY. Vincent...

VINCENT. Somebody's died.

KAY. Who?

(**THOMAS** *freezes.*)

VINCENT. A friend of mine. Thomas.

KAY. I'm so sorry.

VINCENT. He was a coalminer. He used to model for me.

KAY. What happened?

VINCENT. There was a cave-in. He... His wife said in her letter... *(He can't go on.)*

(The lights fade on **THOMAS** *and the coalmining scene.)*

KAY. I'm so sorry, Vincent...

VINCENT. He had a bad leg, a bad back – he shouldn't even have been working that day!

KAY. Vincent, don't –

VINCENT. I told them that mine wouldn't hold! I told them over and over!

KAY. There's nothing you could have done –

VINCENT. I went down there myself. I could see how unsteady it was. I told them.

KAY. They let you go down there?

VINCENT. All they could see was their profits.

KAY. They gave the preacher permission to go – ?

VINCENT. God gave me permission. God demanded that I take care of my flock, and I tried to.

KAY. That's why they fired you?

VINCENT. I tried to tell them, but they wouldn't listen. Now look what's happened.

KAY. Reasonable people respond better to reason than –

VINCENT. Reasonable people would have closed down that mine.

KAY. You shouldn't have put yourself in such danger.

VINCENT. Why not? They have wives and children to support. What do I have?

KAY. You have your family, your work.

VINCENT. Yes…and I would give all of it just to bring back Thomas or any of the others. If I could have just found a way to get through to those pious bastards!

KAY. Well, it's no wonder you weren't able to, with that attitude…

VINCENT. *(throws down his sketchpad)* I'm going back there.

KAY. What?

VINCENT. I'm going back to the coalmines.

KAY. To do what?

VINCENT. If you see a tragedy about to happen, and you can do something to prevent it –

KAY. You've done what you can. You've sacrificed enough.

VINCENT. I did nothing. How can I spend my days putting lines down on paper when there are real human lives that need saving? *(He starts to leave.)*

KAY. Because this is what God intended.

(**VIN** *stops.*)

This is what God wants you to do.

VINCENT. What makes you think so?

KAY. *(bends down, picks up the sketchpad, dusts it off)* I wasn't sure before, but now I am.

VINCENT. How?

KAY. I've always felt a special closeness to you. Beyond being cousins, I mean…as if we shared some sort of secret.

VINCENT. Yes. I felt that way too.

KAY. Then perhaps you can understand how I felt when I heard them all talking about your dismissal from the church…after all the talks we'd had about God and doing His service…

VINCENT. I still believe that, Kay.

KAY. Yes. I can see that.

VINCENT. I look around here and I see Him. So simple, so plain, so real. I feel closer to Him when I'm with you.

(**MAGDA**, *a young peasant woman dressed in dark clothing, enters unseen upstage right. She stands & watches, as* **KAY** *hands* **VINCENT** *the sketchpad. He takes the pad, while holding onto her hands. They look deeply into each other's eyes.*)

KAY. *(shakes her head)* You need almost as much looking after as my child does, don't you?

(**KAY** *and* **VINCENT** *kiss, somewhat shyly.*)

MAGDA. *(giggling)* Look at the pastor's son!

KAY. *(breaks away)* Oh no.

VINCENT. *(to* **MAGDA***)* Move along.

MAGDA. *(to* **VIN***)* I've heard about you.

(**KAY** *hurries off downstage.*)

VINCENT. What are you gawking at? Move off.

MAGDA. *(to* **VIN***)* You're the wild one, aren't you? I'm Magda. You should come visit me.

VINCENT. Move off, I said! Move!

(**MAGDA** *screams, enjoying her terror, exits upstage left.*)

(**VIN** *looks around.*)

Kay? Kay? *(He exits downstage right.)*

(*The lights fade on the clearing, rise on the van Gogh dinner table:* **PASTOR**, **ANNA**, *and* **KAY**. *have their heads bowed in prayer.* **VIN** *rushes in, sits down.*)

PASTOR THEO. Give us grateful hearts, our Father, and let us help those who have less than we do, through Jesus Christ, our Lord. Amen.

(All mumble "Amen," look up. **PASTOR** *looks at* **VINCENT**.*)*

Well. I can't remember the last time you started a meal with the rest of us. To what do we owe this honor?

*(***VINCENT*** *looks at* **KAY**, *smiles.* **KAY** *smiles back.* **ANNA** *smiles at both of them smiling.* **PASTOR** *looks around.)*

So it's Kay's influence, is it?

VINCENT. I'm afraid so.

KAY. No.

ANNA. You make him more sociable.

PASTOR THEO. Yes, I've noticed that too. Please give him as much of that as you can.

KAY. I'll do my best.

PASTOR THEO. So how is the work coming?

VINCENT. In twenty years, I may produce something useful.

PASTOR THEO. I hope it's sooner than that.

ANNA. He's not being serious.

VINCENT. I am.

KAY. Vincent's making wonderful progress. I can see it myself.

ANNA. So can I.

VINCENT. Father? If you hear any rumors from a peasant girl…

PASTOR THEO. What rumors?

KAY. Oh, it was the silliest thing. I was handing Vincent his sketchpad, when a girl from the village came along and made some silly remarks.

PASTOR THEO. What kind of remarks?

KAY. It's too silly even to think about.

ANNA. Exactly. It happens all the time. *(to* **VIN***)* Do you know the girl's name?

(VIN *shakes his head.*)

PASTOR THEO. As you say, it's not even worth thinking about. *(He smiles at* KAY.*)*

(Lights dim on this scene. PASTOR *and* ANNA *move immediately to the study.)*

Scene Three

(Lights rise on **PASTOR THEO** *at his writing table.)*

ANNA. *(enters, holding a piece of paper)* Here's the list of pupils in the Bible Study class, dear. The only one I'm not sure about is Margaret Stoffels. Her mother insists she's enrolled, but she didn't show up for the first meeting, and I've lost any patience –

PASTOR THEO. Anna?

ANNA. Yes dear?

PASTOR THEO. Convince Kay to go back home early.

ANNA. Why?

PASTOR THEO. Tell her it's not good for her child to stay away longer.

ANNA. But she seems to be doing so well here… She and Vincent have gotten so close again.

PASTOR THEO. Yes.

ANNA. Isn't that what you wanted?

PASTOR THEO. It's nothing against Vincent, dear. I just keep thinking about something Kay said…about handing Vincent his sketchpad.

ANNA. Yes?

PASTOR THEO. They're in the middle of the woods… Why wouldn't he be carrying his own sketchpad?

ANNA. I'm sure there are many reasons. He might have been looking at something on the ground, or climbing a tree, or –

PASTOR THEO. I'm sure you're right, dear. I'm sure it's nothing. Will you do as I asked?

ANNA. But it will look as if you don't trust him.

PASTOR THEO. Anna, please. If there was another disaster, I would never get Stricker to help me…

ANNA. Isn't that a chance we have to take? Isn't our family's happiness worth it?

PASTOR THEO. But I cannot be stuck here forever! Not when everyone else in the family has moved on to a place of importance but me, and now – I'm sure God intended something else for me than just this...

ANNA. Fine. I'll tell Kay to leave right away. *(pause)*

PASTOR THEO. Maybe you're right. Christ tells us to believe in Redemption, that it's never too late...

ANNA. Why don't you tell him that, dear?

PASTOR THEO. But how could I...?

ANNA. Just tell him.

(Pause. Then lights fade on the study, rise on **VINCENT** *in his cluttered studio, downstage right, writing by candlelight.* **KAY** *enters and stands by the doorway, wearing a robe and nightdress.* **VINCENT** *doesn't see her.)*

KAY. *(knocks on the door)* Can I come in?

VINCENT. *(flustered)* Kay?

KAY. Am I disturbing you?

VINCENT. *(clears off a chair)* No. I was just writing to Theo.

KAY. It's so good you and Theo are close. It's easy to become distant, even with family.

VINCENT. Yes.

KAY. I hope you're not shocked by my coming here this time of night. I'm sure your parents probably wouldn't approve... I know mine wouldn't...but I was lying in bed, and I just felt so thankful for all your kindness.

VINCENT. Kay, I –

KAY. For the way you've given up so much of your time to help me feel better... Especially when you've suffered a loss yourself.

VINCENT. Kay, you don't have to –

KAY. I'm so glad you stayed here and didn't go back to the coalmines.

VINCENT. Yes.

KAY. I just thought: why shouldn't I come here and tell him? That's something I wouldn't have had the nerve to do – well, certainly not before Friedrich… It's probably silly of me.

VINCENT. No.

KAY. Well, anyway…

(She goes to **VINCENT** *and kisses him on the forehead.)*

Thank you so much. You've been so much more than a cousin to me. I feel like there's nothing I couldn't tell you.

(She smiles at him, then turns and starts to exit.)

VINCENT. Kay?

KAY. *(turns)* Yes?

VINCENT. Would you pose for me?

KAY. Certainly.

VINCENT. Yes?

KAY. We'll take a walk through the fields tomorrow morning…

VINCENT. No. Now.

KAY. Now?

VINCENT. Come over here.

KAY. This is not a good time, Vincent.

VINCENT. Why not?

KAY. I'm not dressed. And I look awful.

VINCENT. You don't.

KAY. Please Vincent.

VINCENT. I see you in a way I never have before…

(He motions for her to sit, and she does.)

KAY. *(fidgeting)* What if your parents come in?

VINCENT. *(getting out his sketchpad and pencil, setting up)* They never come here.

KAY. What if they go to my room and see I'm not there?

VINCENT. Kay – we're not children anymore, are we?

KAY. But think how it would look... As you say, we're not children...

VINCENT. *(sketches)* Your face is such a wonderful shape. Almost a perfect oval. Your features are so alive. You don't know how rare that is. Most women's faces are blanks, they show nothing.

KAY. I'm sure that's not true. You just haven't met the right woman.

VINCENT. Your mouth...your eyes...perfect... *(He sketches.)*

KAY. I've been thinking about what you said to me the other day...about Friedrich.

VINCENT. Friedrich was a very good man.

KAY. Friedrich was a friend of my father's, and I married him to please Papa. *(pause)* Oh. I've never told that to anyone... Friedrich was a wonderful generous man, and he loved me very much, and he gave me a wonderful son – but I never loved him. I didn't. *(pause)* Oh God.

VINCENT. *(puts down the sketchpad)* Kay...

KAY. I'm terrible.

VINCENT. You're not.

KAY. I'm a terrible daughter, a terrible wife and a terrible mother. I was unworthy of Friedrich. Completely unworthy.

VINCENT. *(approaches KAY)* You're very beautiful, Kay...

KAY. I'm awful.

VINCENT. You have a light inside you.

KAY. Wretched and awful.

VINCENT. You have a light inside that shines out – very bright. Almost blinding.

KAY. You mustn't come near me. I am beyond hope.

VINCENT. You give out such a radiance...

KAY. I am a leper. I should be kept apart from civilized people.

VINCENT. There is so much love inside you, Kay. So much love. *(He starts gently stroking her hair.)*

KAY. I am a leper. You mustn't touch me.

(**VIN** *continues stroking her hair.*)

You mustn't do such things, Vincent. Even if it's only the two of us.

VINCENT. So much love… Don't bury it inside you forever…

(*He kisses her.*)

KAY. (*pulls away*) Vincent.

VINCENT. Don't lock it away.

(*He kisses her again.*)

KAY. Oh Vincent.

(**KAY** *gives up resistance, waits to be taken.*)

VINCENT. Marry me, Kay.

KAY. What?

VINCENT. Please marry me.

KAY. You don't know what you're saying.

VINCENT. I do. I want you to marry me.

KAY. Vincent. You don't really mean that…

VINCENT. Please forgive me if I'm saying this badly. But the moments we've spent together…have been the only time in so long that I've felt human…

KAY. Vincent.

VINCENT. I am a leper. Like you. We are two lepers. We should start our own colony.

KAY. Vincent…

VINCENT. But you said it yourself, Kay…

KAY. (*fending him off*) What about your family?

VINCENT. Kay –

KAY. You wouldn't want to hurt them…?

VINCENT. No.

KAY. Then I think I should leave here. (*moving away*)

VINCENT. (*blocks her way*) Marry me.

KAY. Don't do this!

VINCENT. We have so much to give each other.

KAY. We have nothing to give each other!

VINCENT. We do. You said so before…

KAY. Oh Vincent, I don't want to lose you, not now. You are very important to me.

VINCENT. Then marry me.

KAY. No!

VINCENT. Kay. I will never love anyone the way I love you. There is so much inside me…

KAY. No. Do you hear me?

VINCENT. So much I want to show you.

KAY. Don't you understand, we could never –

VINCENT. Don't push me away…

KAY. No. Never. Never. *(She runs from the room)*

VINCENT. *(falls to his knees; softly)* Kay…

> *(Lights fade to black. mining town images, no longer tied to a linear narrative –* **REVEREND PETERSON** *(church overseer) and the miner's wife.)*

REVEREND PETERSON. *(Lutheran preacher)* You are here to communicate God's love, and if you can't do that –

MININGTOWN WOMAN. Preacher Vincent, you say that God loves us. But this is not love!

REVEREND PETERSON. You don't have to make anything up. God's love is recorded right there in the scriptures.

MININGTOWN WOMAN. This is not love!

REVEREND PETERSON. This is His love!

MININGTOWN WOMAN. This is not love!

Scene Four

(Lights up on **THEO** *and* **VINCENT** *in the clearing.)*

THEO. You simply must come to Paris as soon as you can, Vincent. As soon as you feel ready, and we can afford it. There's a group of painters at work there you simply must see.

VINCENT. *(lighting his pipe)* Yes?

THEO. Light seems to radiate from their paintings. Their work seems to *create* light, not just represent it.

VINCENT. That does sound remarkable.

THEO. Oh, you have no idea.

VINCENT. What about my work? What did you think of that last batch of drawings?

THEO. Well...to be perfectly honest...

VINCENT. Which is just how I want you to be...

THEO. The action of your figures wasn't clearly enough expressed. Not articulated fully enough.

VINCENT. Yes exactly. You're right.

THEO. But your landscapes are getting better. I see real progress.

VINCENT. Yes, so do I. I know my stuff is still ugly, still hopelessly ugly, but I feel a power sometimes – do you understand? I can do this. *(pause)* Oh, we're to a great success, Theo. A great success.

THEO. It is possible.

VINCENT. Possible? Possible? Here, look at these. I drew them all since my last letter.
(He hands **THEO** *a sheaf of drawings.)* Do you see how a softer edge has come into the work? Do you see how much stronger my touch is?

THEO. They're better. It's true. I still can't be sure if they're sellable, but –

VINCENT. Oh, damn "sellable"! Who knows what's "sellable"?

THEO. Well, I'm supposed to. That's what they pay me for.

VINCENT. They're good, I just know they are.

THEO. Yes. They're a real improvement.

VINCENT. And do you know why they're good, and why everything is possible now?

THEO. Why?

VINCENT. Because I'm in love.

THEO. What?

VINCENT. I've fallen in love, boy. Can you believe it? This mangy old sheepdog's in love. And I see everything differently now.

THEO. That's wonderful, Vincent. I'm happy for you. Really happy. *(pause)* So who is she? Someone I know?

VINCENT. Yes.

THEO. She must be from the village then...

VINCENT. Well...

THEO. Caroline Roos. I always thought you two made a good match.

VINCENT. Not Caroline.

THEO. Then Clara Fitzwillem?

VINCENT. No.

THEO. Anna Eindhoven? Elizabeth Stoffels?

(VIN *shakes his head.*)

Oh, I know... Helen... What's-her-name, the new teacher –

VINCENT. Not her either, Theo.

THEO. Then who? I'm completely stumped.

(pause)

Oh – is it one of your models?

One of the women you've sketched?

VINCENT. I sketched her, that's true.

THEO. Well, you'll have to help me out then. I don't know most of their names.

VINCENT. You know this one's name.

THEO. I do?

VINCENT. Yes. *(pause)* It's Kay.

THEO. Who?

VINCENT. Kay Vos.

THEO. Our cousin Kay?

VINCENT. Yes.

THEO. You're joking?

VINCENT. Not at all.

THEO. Please Vincent.

VINCENT. I've never felt like this. I've never seen so much beauty, so many shades and colors. I never realized that nature, that life, could be so –

THEO. But she's our cousin! Our mother's sister's daughter.

VINCENT. I know. And I love her.

THEO. Vincent! Just think about this for a moment. *(pause)* Cousin Kay has a small child.

VINCENT. I know.

THEO. Her husband died a short time ago.

VINCENT. Yes. She confided her grief very freely to me.

THEO. Oh? And did you confide in her too?

VINCENT. Yes.

THEO. So you told her your feelings?

VINCENT. That's right.

THEO. And what did she say?

VINCENT. She said no. She said she could never love me that way.

THEO. Really? Well, I think that's for the best.

VINCENT. Do you? Well, I never will, and I'm going to change her.

THEO. Show some common sense please! We're not children anymore, are we?

VINCENT. All I know is I love her, and I will make her love me.

THEO. You can't "make" somebody love you. Either they do or they don't.

VINCENT. She's put a block of ice in my path, but I will melt it.

THEO. Oh Vincent... This is very bad news.

VINCENT. I will melt down that block of ice, Theo. You'll see.

THEO. Have you discussed your feelings with father or mother?

VINCENT. No.

THEO. Well, did Kay say anything to them before she left?

VINCENT. No.

THEO. Then that's fine. Let's just drop the whole thing before it goes any further.

VINCENT. I can't.

THEO. Vincent!

VINCENT. She has so much life in her, Theo. So much warmth, so much love... I can't let her waste it.

THEO. There's nothing more you can do.

VINCENT. I'm going to Amsterdam, and I will change her.

THEO. You'll ruin everything, Vincent. Everything we've been building up.

VINCENT. Oh Theo, if you were in love –

THEO. Well I'm not. Thank God one of us isn't.

VINCENT. If you knew how this feeling can change you, can transform the world, re-make all creation! I walked past the bakery yesterday, and I suddenly saw what a magnificent structure it was...the same bakery I've seen all my life, but now it was five in the morning, and the smoke was coming out of the chimney, and the loaves of bread were being stacked, and there was such love there – such love! – that I couldn't walk any further, I had to sit down and let the warmth of that love just wash over me... And I suddenly understood the miracle of bread in the Bible, it wasn't a parable, no! Jesus made that bread from his flesh, it was really his flesh, and that's what I want our painting to be,

I want to feed thousands, to give them our body, our blood, and all of our soul, to give everything! Hold nothing back! Hold nothing back.

THEO. Vincent… I don't want to see you get hurt.

VINCENT. But I feel so protected now, Theo… Even the piles of rubble down by the dump look full of mystery these days… I went down there this morning and turned out a whole batch of sketches, and I think it's some of the best work I've done. (VIN *flips through his sketchpad.*)

THEO. Not now, Vincent.

VINCENT. Oh Theo… What it must be like to wake up in the morning next to someone you love! And then to come home at night, after working all day, and to look in those eyes – the eyes of someone who loves you and needs you…oh God, that would be paradise!

THEO. And what if she never returns your love?

VINCENT. Then I will never marry. That's it. In any case, I'm telling father tonight and leaving for Amsterdam tomorrow. *(starts to exit)*

THEO. I'm begging you, for the sake of what we're doing together as brothers…think of the paintings, will you? The work that we're making together.

(**VINCENT** *starts to exit again.* **THEO***'s tone changes.*)

What about the train to Amsterdam? You don't have money, do you?

VINCENT. *(stops)* No.

THEO. And where were you planning to stay when you got there? Or do you think Uncle Stricker will be so happy to see you that he'll put you up in his house?

VINCENT. I was hoping you'd help me with money. *(pause)* But if you won't, I understand. I will manage.

THEO. How?

VINCENT. I've managed before.

THEO. Vincent: I'll give you the money if you promise to wait a few days and think this over…

VINCENT. I can't.

THEO. Just wait a week and see how you feel. Talk things over with father and mother, then –

VINCENT. No.

THEO. I'm sure Cousin Kay would find you far more persuasive in a calm frame of mind –

VINCENT. Damn you! Don't lecture me. Either give me the money or don't.

THEO. Allright then! I'll give you the money on one condition: come back right away to the parsonage if she turns you down. *(pause)* Right away, okay? Just accept it like a man if it happens, and –

VINCENT. *(warning him)* Theo.

THEO. *(looks at watch)* I have a little more than an hour before my train leaves… I'll talk to father about this. I know he won't like it, but… Hopefully, by this time next week it will all be resolved.

VINCENT. I will talk to father myself.

THEO. Vincent. Please. Let me just come in the room with you.

VINCENT. No.

THEO. Don't make it impossible to come back here. There's nowhere else for you to go now, and –

VINCENT. *(holds up his hand)* We're going to be all right, don't worry. We'll have our success, whatever happens.

(Lights fade on the clearing, rise on the parsonage livingroom: **PASTOR THEO** *is reading the newspaper,* **ANNA** *is knitting.)*

PASTOR THEO. *(reading aloud)* Listen to this: "The children of Cape Town run wild during the day, some of them clothed in torn shirts or rags, otherwise entirely naked…"

*(*VINCENT *enters.* PASTOR *looks up briefly, then reads:)*

PASTOR THEO. *(cont.)* "Their parents seemed unconcerned, and actually encouraged this savagery before Reverend Caufield and I told them in no uncertain terms" –

VINCENT. *(stands awkwardly)* Father?

PASTOR THEO. Just a minute. "…in no uncertain terms that this was outside the bounds of decent behavior, and could not be tolerated – "

VINCENT. Father?

ANNA. Your father is reading now, Vincent. Come over and sit next to me.

(**VINCENT** *sits down next to* **ANNA.** **ANNA** *absently strokes the back of his neck)*

PASTOR THEO. *(searching)* "outside the bounds of…" Oh yes – "And could not be tolerated in a civilized society." Can you believe that? These creatures are ignorant of the most basic –

VINCENT. *(blurts out)* Maybe they're better off that way.

PASTOR THEO. What?

ANNA. Your father's just making a point, dear.

PASTOR THEO. These people dwell in darkness, in total darkness, you can't deny that.

VINCENT. So now they're no longer "creatures" but "people"?

PASTOR THEO. You know what I meant.

VINCENT. Yes.

PASTOR THEO. The Church is their beacon, their light in the darkness.

VINCENT. We've come to bring them the hope of salvation.

PASTOR THEO. That is very well put. I remember when you believed it yourself.

VINCENT. God save them from our "salvation."

ANNA. *(to* **PASTOR***)* I think that would make an excellent theme for a sermon, don't you? About the Church being their light in the darkness…

PASTOR THEO. We could combine it with another clothing drive. *(folds the paper)* Time to go upstairs.

ANNA. Wasn't there something you wanted to tell Vincent?

PASTOR THEO. What? Oh... *(turns to* **VIN***)* We just want you to know that we're very proud of you, boy. I was a bit skeptical at first, I must admit, but – you seem to be making great strides. Everyone says so. And so...well... let's hope the worst is behind you.

ANNA. We're both very grateful for all the time you spent here with Kay... I think you gave her great comfort.

PASTOR THEO. I just can't help feeling you would've made a great minister, boy. If circumstances had been different, I mean. But I guess everything turned out for the best... *(goes up to* **VIN***)* Thank you for all your help. We are very grateful.

(He shakes **VINCENT***'s hand.)*

ANNA. We really are, Vincent.

(She kisses **VIN***.)*

*(***PASTOR THEO** *starts to leave the room.)*

VINCENT. Father?

PASTOR THEO. *(stops, turns)* Yes, boy?

VINCENT. There's something we need to talk over.

PASTOR THEO. Can't it wait till tomorrow?

VINCENT. I'm afraid not.

ANNA. I'll leave the room if you want me to.

VINCENT. No, I think you should stay.

*(***PASTOR** *and* **ANNA** *exchange a glance, sit.)*

PASTOR THEO. So what is it, boy? What's on your mind?

VINCENT. I'm...going to Amsterdam tomorrow.

PASTOR THEO. So suddenly? Why?

VINCENT. I just have to go.

PASTOR THEO. Are you going there to see other artists?

VINCENT. I would like to see other painters, yes... But that's not why I'm going.

PASTOR THEO. Good. Because you could do that at any time.

ANNA. You're going to see Kay, aren't you?

VINCENT. Yes.

ANNA. Oh Vincent, please… *(She stands and moves toward* **VIN.***)*

PASTOR THEO. Kay? But she was just here.

VINCENT. I'm sorry, mother. I have to.

ANNA. You don't.

PASTOR THEO. Can't you write her a letter?

VINCENT. There are some things that cannot be put in a letter.

PASTOR THEO. Like what?

ANNA. Think about what you're doing here, Vincent. Think very clearly about what you're doing…

VINCENT. I am.

ANNA. There is a line that cannot be crossed. There is a line.

PASTOR THEO. What are you two gabbing about? What kind of "line?"

ANNA. Vincent knows what I mean. Don't you?

VINCENT. Yes.

PASTOR THEO. Well I don't. *(to* **VIN***)* Why are you in such a terrible rush?

ANNA. You don't want to know, Theodorus.

PASTOR THEO. I do, and I demand to be told.

ANNA. Let's go upstairs.

PASTOR THEO. I will not. I don't know what's gotten into the two of you tonight, but there will be no more displays, do you hear me? Now tell me what's going on.

VINCENT. *(softly)* I'm in love with Kay.

PASTOR THEO. What?

VINCENT. I'm in love with Kay.

PASTOR THEO. Of course you love Kay. She's your cousin.

ANNA. He doesn't mean that kind of love.

PASTOR THEO. What?

VINCENT. I've asked her to marry me.

PASTOR THEO. Oh Lord.

ANNA. *(to* **VIN***)* Now are you happy?

PASTOR THEO. Please God, tell me it's not true…

VINCENT. It is, and it's a good thing, you'll see.

PASTOR THEO. *(to* **ANNA***)* Didn't I tell you about that sketchpad!

ANNA. I never suspected anything!

VINCENT. *(to* **PASTOR***)* Don't yell at her!

PASTOR THEO. Didn't I tell you? Didn't I? Why couldn't you listen?

VINCENT. Yell at me, if you want to! Not her!

(**PASTOR THEO** *suddenly staggers, almost falling down.*)

ANNA. Theodorus!

(*She holds on, steadies him;* **VINCENT** *helps.*)

PASTOR THEO. *(points to a chair)* Just get me to… Help me…

(**ANNA** *and* **VINCENT** *help him to sit down.*)

VINCENT. Are you alright, father? Should I get you a doctor?

(**PASTOR** *shakes his head.*)

ANNA. *(turns on* **VIN***)* Why did you have to do this?

VINCENT. Believe me, I wish I didn't.

ANNA. She refused you, of course.

VINCENT. Yes.

ANNA. No wonder you were siding with the savages before. You're a savage yourself.

VINCENT. Yes.

ANNA. You're no better than one of them!

VINCENT. That's right.

PASTOR THEO. *(regaining control)* That's enough now.

ANNA. Here we have loved you, and given you everything –

PASTOR THEO. Enough, I said! There will be no more discussion, because there is nothing more to discuss. No one is going to Amsterdam, and nothing more will be said on the subject.

VINCENT. I am going.

ANNA. Damn you!

PASTOR THEO. Anna!

ANNA. Why are you trying to hurt him?

VINCENT. I don't want to hurt anyone.

PASTOR THEO. You're not speaking with Kay, and that's final. God knows what damage you've already done.

ANNA. Listen to your father, please...

VINCENT. I have no choice here.

PASTOR THEO. Then there is something wrong with you, boy. Something terribly terribly wrong.

ANNA. *(pulling him back)* Theodorus...

PASTOR THEO. If you go through with this, boy...then you will never set foot in this house again. Do you hear me, Lord? Never! *(to* **VIN***)* The decision is yours. It is all up to you.

(Pause. **VINCENT** *rushes off stage left.* **PASTOR** *and* **ANNA** *look after him. Lights fade on the parsonage.)*

Scene Five

(Lights up immediately down right: vanity table with mirror and chair. KAY stands in a white nightdress, leaning on the back of a chair, tensely clutches a hairbrush. A MAID enters.)

KAY. Well?

MAID. He still won't leave, Madame.

KAY. Why not?

MAID. He says he has to see you.

KAY. But did you tell him I can't?

MAID. He said that he doesn't mind waiting, no matter how long…

KAY. *(Pause: she paces.)* Oh Vincent. Is this my fault? What can I tell you?

MAID. I'm sure that everything will be fine as soon as Reverend Stricker returns home –

KAY. No!

MAID. Madame?

KAY. That must not happen.

MAID. Begging your pardon, Madame, but –

KAY. Don't you see? I will have to explain to him how – How this could… What could I say? How could I ever explain it?

MAID. *(perplexed)* Madame?

(Lights fade on this, rise downstage left on a table & chair, VINCENT pacing. He takes out a sketchpad and pencil, sits.)

VINCENT. You have to see me. You have to see me. You have to see me.

(Pause: he closes his eyes. Then he opens them and starts sketching KAY from memory. A few moments pass. KAY enters, carrying a lit candle.)

(VIN looks up.) Thank God.

KAY. *(puts the candle down on the table)* Don't come any closer. Please.

(She puts out her hands: **VINCENT** *takes them.)*

I forgive you.

VINCENT. What?

KAY. I forgive you, Vincent. Let's never lose our heads again. Alright? Let's be friends forever. *(She smiles.)* You'll join us for supper tomorrow, won't you? I'm sure father and mother will be happy to see you.

VINCENT. Kay, please, I –

KAY. It's late now and I'm rather tired. You must be too. *(She withdraws her hands, backs away.)*

VINCENT. You don't have to be afraid, Kay. *(He extends his hand toward her.)*

KAY. Vincent… I'm giving you the chance to apologize.

VINCENT. We have nothing to apologize for… I'm taking you out of this house of darkness…

KAY. Please stay away from me.

VINCENT. Kay…

KAY. Please respect my wishes and keep your distance.

VINCENT. Don't talk to me like a stranger.

KAY. But we are strangers in many ways.

VINCENT. No.

KAY. Who do you think I am? You don't know me.

VINCENT. Oh, but I do. I know just who you are…and who you can be.

KAY. No.

VINCENT. Who we could be, Kay.

KAY. There is no "we," Vincent. There can't be.

VINCENT. *(holds out his hand)* Just feel the strength here, the power…

KAY. Don't do this.

VINCENT. I can take you anywhere you want to go, Kay… I can show you anything…

KAY. Please…leave now…

VINCENT. It's so easy to kill something, Kay… If you leave me now, I will kill it… I will kill our love.

(VINCENT holds his painting hand near the candle flame.)

KAY. Vincent…

VINCENT. There is so much I want to show you… So much beauty… It's ours…

KAY. I can't. I can't do it.

VINCENT. Kay.

(He plunges his hand in the flame, crying out. KAY watches in horror, transfixed. VINCENT and KAY go into shadow as the unfinished "Potato Eaters" is again rear-projected on the screen.)

(The stage goes black.)

End of Act I

ACT II

Scene One

(In front of the scrim: Lights up on an attic room in a run-down section of Amsterdam, furnished only with a few tables and chairs, an old chest of drawers, a washboard & basin, and a screen in back hiding the bedroom. It is night, six weeks after the end of Act I. VINCENT sits at a wobbly wooden table, reworking a sketch: his sketching hand is lightly bandaged, and the work does not go well, but he persists, working by a flickering candle beside him.)

(There's an unlit kerosene lamp on another table.)

(THEO walks in and stands near the door, watching VINCENT.)

VINCENT. *(without looking up)* Hello Theo.

THEO. Hello.

VINCENT. I've been expecting you.

VINCENT. Why don't you pull up a chair? Make yourself comfortable.

THEO. Why are you working in the dark? Can't you get any more light in here?

VINCENT. Yes.

THEO. Well, why don't you?

VINCENT. Because I don't choose to… But if it makes such a difference…

(VIN stands, goes to the other table, picks up matches and lights the lamp – with some problem, owing to his bandage.)

Is that better?

THEO. Yes. *(He walks a few steps closer.)* How is your hand?

VINCENT. Much better.

THEO. Are you seeing a doctor?

VINCENT. I was a doctor of sorts, remember?

THEO. You know what I mean.

VINCENT. And I'm telling you that my experience in the mining camp prepared me very well to dress my own wounds. So you see, I did learn something there after all. *(He sits again.)*

THEO. *(approaching)* Let me see it.

*(He advances quickly and touches **VIN**'s hand, trying to get a good look; **VINCENT** cries out, pulls his hand back.)*

I'm sorry. Did that hurt?

VINCENT. No. You – surprised me.

THEO. I didn't mean to. *(pause)* And you can make use of it?

VINCENT. The doctor I saw here – yes, I did see a doctor – said all feeling should be coming back soon.

THEO. But you didn't do anything permanent?

*(**VINCENT** shakes his head.)*

Thank God. You don't know how scared I was, Vincent. When I heard what had happened – and then I didn't hear anything from you…

VINCENT. It wasn't easy to write.

THEO. You could have sent me your address. I think I deserved that much, don't you? *(pause)*
How could you, Vincent?

VINCENT. Don't ask me that, please.

THEO. How could you hurt yourself like that?

VINCENT. It wasn't something I planned.

THEO. Do you have any idea what you did to Kay? I mean, the sight of blood is a terrible event in her life. But to see someone she knows –

VINCENT. Yes, yes, yes –

THEO. To smell your burning flesh and hear you proclaiming your love for her –

VINCENT. That's enough.

THEO. I don't think she's ever going out again. Ever.

VINCENT. I'm glad you find it so funny. *(pause)*

THEO. *(looks around)* So what kind of place is this anyway?

VINCENT. It's a room.

THEO. Whose room?

VINCENT. Does it matter?

THEO. It does to me.

VINCENT. Well then – it's my room.

THEO. Oh yes? Since when did you start taking in laundry?

VINCENT. Since my brother could not sell my work.

THEO. Don't start with me. There's no point…

VINCENT. You're quite right. There isn't. *(He sketches.)*

THEO. Vincent – I don't have much time here.

VINCENT. Of course you don't. None of us do.

THEO. Can we end this charade now?

VINCENT. My pleasure.

THEO. You wrote me a letter, remember? I have your money.

VINCENT. Yes? But you could have saved yourself some bother and sent it.

THEO. Goddamnit, Vincent, I – I haven't slept for a month, worrying about where you were, and how you were – But your painting hand. What were you thinking?

(He walks over to **VINCENT***, cradling his bandaged hand.)*

This hand is more important to me than… Promise me you'll never do that again.

VINCENT. It's not the kind of thing I'd like to do twice.

THEO. If you feel the urge coming on, then hit me, all right? Put *my* hand in a fire. Do anything, just as long as you give me your solemn oath that you'll never –

SIEN. *(offstage; behind the screen, waking up)* Vincent?

VINCENT. Yes?

SIEN. *(offstage)* I thought I heard voices.

VINCENT. You did. My brother's come for a visit.

SIEN. *(offstage)* Your brother? Oh yes.

THEO. So: you haven't been suffering all alone?

VINCENT. *(to SIEN)* Come out and meet him.

SIEN. *(offstage)* Just a minute.

THEO. *(to VIN)* You're more resourceful than I thought.

VINCENT. Thank you.

THEO. I can leave now, if you'd like me to…

VINCENT. No. I want you to meet her.

THEO. *(primping)* Oh yes? And what is her name?

VINCENT. Sien. *(pronounced "seen")*

THEO. "Seen?" That's unusual.

VINCENT. Well, she's an unusual woman. She's helped me –

THEO. Yes, I'm sure she has. I'm glad to see you've come to your senses about Kay. *(mocking)* "Oh, I love her. Her and no other." This is more like it.

VINCENT. Is it?

THEO. Let me give you a little advice from my own experience – which, by the way, is pretty extensive –

(SIEN, 27, emerges from behind the screen. She wears a soiled housedress, her face is still puffy from sleep and her hair is quite wild, but she has a very sensual quality that makes an impression.)

VINCENT. *(leads her forward)* Sien, this is my brother Theo. Theo, this is Sien.

THEO. *(bowing slightly)* My pleasure.

SIEN. Vincent's told me a lot about you.

THEO. *(to VIN)* Have you really? But why?

SIEN. He says he could never have gotten along…

THEO. I'm sure that's not true.

SIEN. Oh, it must be, or he wouldn't say it. And he's right, you're a very nice dresser.

THEO. Thank you. I suppose I do have a slight weakness for clothes.

SIEN. If you ever want anything washed, I'd be happy to…

THEO. Oh. So this is your room?

SIEN. Yes. Well, mine and Vincent's now.

THEO. Really? How interesting.

VINCENT. So far I haven't kept up my half. Sien has been very generous…

THEO. *(to* **SIEN***)* And that's what you do? You wash clothes.

SIEN. I'm not very good yet.

THEO. I'm sure that's not true.

SIEN. I never really tried until Vincent…

> *(***SIEN*** reaches her hands back for* **VIN***, off-balance.* **VINCENT** *quickly steps up and catches her.)*

It takes some getting used to, but it's better than being out on the streets.

THEO. Oh yes. I'm sure it is. Vincent? *(motions to* **VIN** *that he'd like to speak privately)*

VINCENT. She's really been making progress. Even in this short time –

THEO. *(motions again)* Vincent. *(***SIEN*** yawns.)* Look: we're keeping the lady up.

SIEN. No. I'm used to it from my youngest. Shall I heat up some coffee?

THEO. Your youngest?

SIEN. My boy Paul. He's ten months.

THEO. Oh?

VINCENT. She has three children.

THEO. Does she?

VINCENT. She's done an incredible job, considering…

THEO. And where is the father?

SIEN. I'm afraid you mean "father*s*."

THEO. Do I?

VINCENT. It's the old story. As soon as they heard she was pregnant, they left.

SIEN. Just like all men. Except Vincent, of course.

THEO. Oh?

VINCENT. *(to SIEN)* There's still some wine left.

SIEN. Why didn't I think of that? We'll have a party. *(She goes after wine and glasses.)*

THEO. *(motions again)* Vincent?

VINCENT. *(joins him this time)* Yes?

THEO. What's going on here?

VINCENT. What do you think?

THEO. Have you gotten her pregnant?

VINCENT. No.

THEO. Well, thank God for that. How could you get so intimate with this woman?

VINCENT. She saved my life.

THEO. Oh yes?

VINCENT. I was wandering the streets, half out of my mind, my hand throbbing with pain, and she − *(He stops.)*

THEO. Vincent: it's clear that she's using you.

VINCENT. Is it? Well, I'd like to marry her.

THEO. What?

SIEN. *(pouring the wine)* It's all ready, whenever you are…

VINCENT. *(to SIEN)* That's good.

THEO. *(to VIN)* You're not really serious?

VINCENT. Very.

THEO. But you were dying to marry Kay.

VINCENT. I need love, Theo, real human love. Do you understand? I cannot live without it.

THEO. You're just being melodramatic now.

VINCENT. Is it melodramatic to eat, to breathe?

THEO. But take a good look at her, Vincent.

VINCENT. We have something to give each other.

THEO. I'm sure.

VINCENT. And she's an excellent model, you'll see. We work well together.

THEO. I have no doubt.

VINCENT. *(raising his glass)* I think we should propose a toast.

SIEN. Oh yes, let's!

VINCENT. Why don't you give the toast, brother?

THEO. *(looks at his watch)* I'm afraid I have to go.

SIEN. No.

VINCENT. Just stay and have one glass with us.

SIEN. Please do.

THEO. I'm sorry. It's been very good meeting you. Vincent? *(He motions again.)*

VINCENT. No Theo.

THEO. Right now.

VINCENT. We have no secrets here. You can say whatever you need to in front of Sien.

THEO. Oh? *(He looks at SIEN.)*

SIEN. If you need to talk privately…

VINCENT. No. *(to THEO)* Go ahead.

THEO. *(to SIEN)* I don't know if my brother's informed you, but our father is a prominent clergyman whose reputation has already been damaged… If your arrangement should ever be made public –

VINCENT. We're getting married, I told you.

THEO. That would be much worse.

VINCENT. Why?

THEO. You're driving him to disown you.

VINCENT. He's already banished me.

THEO. He's trying to find a way to forgive you.

VINCENT. What makes you so sure?

SIEN. *(breaks in)* No! I don't want you to argue. Not over me.

VINCENT. This has nothing to do with you.

SIEN. Doesn't it?

THEO. The lady is right: let's not argue. *(to SIEN)* I'm only sorry I had to speak harshly.

SIEN. I understand.

VINCENT. No you don't. *(to THEO)* I'm not leaving here.

THEO. As you wish.

VINCENT. And my palette is getting darker, not lighter. You can't imagine how dark.

THEO. You're doing this just to spite me.

VINCENT. I'm doing portraits of working-folk here –

THEO. If you just came to Paris –

VINCENT. I'll come when I'm ready.

THEO. I have a stake in this too.

VINCENT. But I'm doing the painting. *(pause)*

THEO. *(puts money order in VIN's hand)* Do not marry her, Vincent.

VINCENT. You don't really know her.

THEO. Do not.

(He nods politely to SIEN, then exits. Pause.)

SIEN. Silly to let his wine go to waste... *(She drinks THEO's wine.)* How much is it?

VINCENT. What?

SIEN. The money. *(SIEN looks)* It would take me three weeks on my back to make this.

VINCENT. Don't talk like that.

SIEN. What?

VINCENT. Like a whore.

SIEN. Isn't that what I am?

VINCENT. No. That's what you were.

SIEN. *(holds up money order)* And what about you? What is this for?

VINCENT. For paints.

SIEN. Oh. And it looked like a payment to me.

VINCENT. I am no –

> (**SIEN** *laughs.*)

SIEN. *(picks up wine bottle)* I've been a kept woman too, you know. I know how it feels.

> *(She swigs the wine, starts walking toward the screen.* **VINCENT** *grabs her.)*

VINCENT. We were doing fine before this. We were doing so well.

SIEN. Were we?

VINCENT. Don't let my brother poison your mind with his Parisian snobbery.

SIEN. He woke me up, that's all. I was dreaming.

VINCENT. Then go back to sleep.

SIEN. Oh, I'll sleep again, but I won't dream. I know who I am now.

> *(She pulls* **VINCENT** *down, kisses him with a whore's kiss.* **VINCENT** *grabs her and pushes her away.)*

VINCENT. Don't do that. Don't fall back. You're better than that.

SIEN. What if I'm not?

VINCENT. I love you. I want to marry you.

SIEN. You want to make me "respectable"?

VINCENT. Didn't you hear me? I love you.

SIEN. I understand.

VINCENT. No you don't. We can make a life together.

SIEN. Yes, Vincent.

VINCENT. Believe me, if we let the world tell us who we are, then we'd all be whores.

> (**SIEN** *blows him a kiss, then vanishes behind the screen.)*

VINCENT. Sien? I haven't finished with you. *(pause)* We want the same thing, don't we?

> *(Pause.* **VINCENT** *follows her off. Lights fade to black.)*

Scene Two

(In the garden in back of the van Gogh parsonage, spring 1884 – two years after the end of Act I. **ANNA** *stands, wearing a kitchen apron over her clothes.* **PASTOR THEO** *is on his knees, weeding the garden. He wears some kind of outer garment to protect his clothing.)*

ANNA. It's getting cold, Theodorus. Why don't you do this another day?

PASTOR THEO. I've let it go too long as it is.

ANNA. A few days either way…

PASTOR THEO. *(pulling weeds)* "Don't put off till tomorrow"… that's what my father always said. *(weeding)* Anyway this will help me think.

ANNA. Let's try not to argue this time. Let's try to be a family, all right?

PASTOR THEO. If Vincent wants to be eccentric, so be it. I just hope the parishioners understand.

ANNA. I think they do. They accept it. And there will be no more talk of that other thing, will there? You promise me? *(pause:* **PASTOR** *nods)*

He really wants to come back. That's what Theo says. He's really changed now.

PASTOR THEO. I suppose we'll find out soon enough… *(pause)*

ANNA. *(removes her apron)* I'm going into the village now, dear. Is there anything I can get you?

PASTOR THEO. Are you sure there's time?

ANNA. He isn't due for three hours.

*(***PASTOR** *nods, goes back to weeding.* **ANNA** *looks at him with concern, then goes over, kisses him on the forehead.)*

PASTOR THEO. What was that for?

ANNA. I think you're a very great man.

PASTOR THEO. Ha. Tell it to the clerical board.

ANNA. *(shaking her head)* I'm so glad I married you.

(ANNA exits through door **SR. PASTOR THEO** *continues weeding.)*

*(***VINCENT*** *enters stage left, carrying a bag, his painting equipment slung over his shoulder. He is dressed in a fur hat, old soldier's tunic, workman's pants and old shoes, everything splattered with paint. He stands for a moment, watches* **PASTOR.***)*

PASTOR THEO. *(senses something, looks around)* Vincent?

VINCENT. *(very gentle)* Hello father.

PASTOR THEO. But… You're not supposed to arrive for another… *(looks at his watch)*

VINCENT. I took an earlier train.

PASTOR THEO. But – How –

VINCENT. I got out at Zundert and walked.

PASTOR THEO. That's over 12 miles!

VINCENT. The countryside was even more beautiful than I remembered…

(He takes the painting equipment off his shoulder.)

I'd like to take a look at my studio…

PASTOR THEO. Vincent?

VINCENT. Yes?

PASTOR THEO. I don't want to fight anymore.

VINCENT. Good. Neither do I. I never did.

PASTOR THEO. But that never stopped us.

VINCENT. No. *(pause)*

PASTOR THEO. Whatever happened in the past is the past… I really mean that.

VINCENT. Good. So do I.

PASTOR THEO. I guess you know that I had some hopes of getting a larger parish. Now that's in the past too.

VINCENT. I'm sorry, father.

PASTOR THEO. I'm just a country preacher, that's all. That's just how God meant it to be. *(pause)* What's important to me now is my peace. I want everything peaceful. Do you understand?

VINCENT. Yes.

PASTOR THEO. I'd like to believe that human beings, especially if they share the same blood, can live in peace with each other. Now this may be just another illusion on my part, but I'd like to preserve it.

VINCENT. All right.

PASTOR THEO. I think you'll find when you get older that sometimes illusions are better than truths. I know A pastor is not supposed to say that, but... *(pause)* But you do whatever you need to. I'm not trying to change you.

VINCENT. No more rules?

PASTOR THEO. What? Oh no. Only...

VINCENT. Yes?

PASTOR THEO. Try not to stir up the village too much. Let's not give those Catholics any more ammunition...

VINCENT. Does that mean you expect me at services?

PASTOR THEO. That is up to you. Salvation is voluntary, you know that. I cannot save you. You will always be welcome, of course, if you choose to join us. Otherwise...

VINCENT. I don't intend going anywhere near a church, or near respectable townspeople.

PASTOR THEO. If that's what you've decided.

VINCENT. I only want to paint peasants. Peasants and country landscapes, that's all. Before they disappear.

PASTOR THEO. Oh? And where are they going?

VINCENT. The way of all simple things, I'm afraid. They'll soon be swallowed up by machines.

PASTOR THEO. Well, that sounds a bit simple-minded, if you don't mind my saying so... These things have been here for ages, and I'm sure they'll continue to be... But you've seen more of the world than me, haven't you? Perhaps you're right, perhaps we're all on the verge of extinction. Who knows? I'm just an old country pastor. Just an old country pastor, that's all...

*(**PASTOR** goes back to weeding. **VINCENT** takes out sketchbook, starts drawing.)*

*(Lights fade on the garden, rise on peasant woman – **MAGDA** – in her hut, peeling potatoes. She wears a white peasant cap that covers her head and a brown dress made of rough material that leaves only her hands uncovered. **VINCENT** turns his attention to her, closing sketchbook, going to an easel that is already set up Downstage. He turns down the brightness of an oil lamp by **MAGDA**'s side.)*

MAGDA. What are you doing?

VINCENT. *(lighting his pipe)* It was too bright in here.

MAGDA. That's how I like it. *(She turns the lamp up again.)*

VINCENT. Magda…

MAGDA. Yes sir?

VINCENT. I would like to see how it looks with less light.

MAGDA. You have already seen.

VINCENT. Magda…

MAGDA. Yes sir?

VINCENT. Please turn down the light.

*(**MAGDA** gives him a look; then reaches over, shuts off light: total darkness.)*

VINCENT. Magda?

MAGDA. Yes sir?

VINCENT. Please kindle the light again.

MAGDA. But I thought you wanted it off.

VINCENT. You know just what I wanted.

*(He strikes a match, walks over to the lamp, rekindles it, adjusts the level; then he returns to his easel. When his back is turned, **MAGDA** raises the level again.)*

Magda!

MAGDA. I'm sorry sir, but I'm used to it a certain way, and that's how it will be. *(She peels potatoes, agitated.)* Why is this so important?

VINCENT. Because it is. I'm a painter, remember?

MAGDA. So?

VINCENT. So a painting is a battleground of light and darkness. The darkness is strong and tries to devour the light, but the light keeps on flickering, refusing to yield, until… *(pause)* I have this idea for a painting. The biggest painting I've ever done.

MAGDA. Yes?

VINCENT. It will be a family at supper… A family of people just like yourself, who've always lived close to the earth. A smoky scent fills the shack, as they dine on potatoes their own hands have picked… The darkness is thick, pierced only by a single lamp…

MAGDA. But you don't want me to cut myself, do you?

VINCENT. Could we lower it somewhat? *(Pause. Then* **MAGDA** *lowers the level slightly.)*

And you can stop calling me "sir." Just "Vincent" is fine.

MAGDA. But that wouldn't be right. You're the pastor's son.

VINCENT. Let's try to forget that for now.

MAGDA. But I can't.

VINCENT. Oh, I think if you try –

MAGDA. *(cries out)* Ow!

VINCENT. What happened?

MAGDA. *(holds up her cut finger)* Now look what you made me do! *(She sucks off the blood.)*

VINCENT. *(stands)* That's all right. Let's bandage it up.

(He reaches in his pocket, takes out a clean handkerchief, walks over to **MAGDA** *and bandages her finger.)*

MAGDA. You do that very well.

VINCENT. Thank you. I've had some practice.

MAGDA. I don't know what to make of you, pastor's son. You're not what I expected.

VINCENT. So I've been told.

MAGDA. *(looks at her finger)* But now I can't peel potatoes, and Mama will kill me if –

VINCENT. Fine. I'll peel the potatoes. *(takes her place on the stool)* Just as long as you follow my instructions from now on. *(He peels potatoes.)*

MAGDA. *(stands, very angelic now)* I promise.

VINCENT. Good. *(He keeps peeling.)*

MAGDA. *(enjoys watching)* You do that very well for a pastor's son.

VINCENT. You don't have a very high opinion of pastor's sons, do you?

MAGDA. Some of us do all the work...

VINCENT. And some of us don't?

MAGDA. That's what Mama says anyway... *(pause)* Have you gone anywhere? Have you traveled?

VINCENT. I've been to a few places, yes.

MAGDA. Big cities?

(VIN nods.)

You see? I've never been anywhere, and I never will.

VINCENT. You don't know that.

MAGDA. I do. When the world was created, God said, "Magda will never go anywhere." Oh, I'm sorry. That's blasphemy, isn't it? I didn't mean to –

(VINCENT waves off her apology.)

You should be angry with me. I sinned against God.

VINCENT. I'm not angry.

MAGDA. You are very strange for a pastor's son, aren't you? *(pause)* Here, let me do that.

VINCENT. I'll be finished soon.

MAGDA. I will do it.

(She takes the knife from him, resumes working.)

So why do you spend your time like this? Can't you do anything useful?

VINCENT. I'm afraid not.

MAGDA. And why haven't you taken a wife yet? You'll be an old man soon.

VINCENT. That's true.

MAGDA. You don't want to grow old all alone, do you? You want to have children?

VINCENT. Now, if we can get back to the painting…

MAGDA. I think you should know there's a lot of talk in the village about you…

VINCENT. *(lowers the light)* I would like to get on with my work now. *(He returns to the easel, etc.)*

MAGDA. I only think you should know because –

VINCENT. Magda please. You promised that you would help me.

(Pause. He dips his brush in the palette, starts making a few strokes.)

MAGDA. I just think it's unfair because –

VINCENT. Magda…

MAGDA. *(stands)* You're not what they say you are, not at all…

VINCENT. *(very commanding)* Sit down.

(Pause. Then MAGDA sits and starts working again.)

Thank you, Magda. *(He paints.)*

MAGDA. *(peels potatoes)* Whatever happened to that woman who was here years ago?

VINCENT. What woman?

MAGDA. That nice-looking woman from the city.

(VINCENT works.)

Always dressed in black, walking around with her nose in the air. You followed her around like a lapdog. *(pause)* Oh, I'm so sorry. I shouldn't talk like that, should I?

VINCENT. *(painting well now)* You can talk however you'd like.

MAGDA. Mama says I'm wicked sometimes. She says it's because I don't have someone steady. I shouldn't be telling this to a pastor's son, should I? *(pause)* Have you seen Mama's bed?

VINCENT. *(not really listening)* Please – no sudden movements.

MAGDA. Oh, it would make a good painting. She has a very soft bed. Not like mine. *(pause)* She won't be back for a while…

VINCENT. Stay still.

MAGDA. Let me show you Mama's bed, Vincent.

VINCENT. What?

MAGDA. *(stands, holds out her hands)* Let me show you Mama's bed.

VINCENT. Sit down.

MAGDA. *(comes toward him)* You're from the country too, aren't you?

VINCENT. Magda! Please!

MAGDA. We're better than those girls from the city…

(She takes **VIN**'s *hand, pulling him offstage.)*

VINCENT. *(pulls away)* Goddamnit! This is impossible!

MAGDA. What?

VINCENT. This is what happens when you don't have trained models!

MAGDA. So you don't like me? I'm not good enough?

VINCENT. No. *(He takes down his canvas, collapses his easel, etc.)*

MAGDA. You prefer girls from the city…

VINCENT. At least they can sit still!

MAGDA. You're just a pastor's son after all, aren't you?

VINCENT. You've wasted enough of my time… *(He storms out.)*

*(***MAGDA*** reaches over and raises the light to its highest level, looks off defiantly in the direction that* **VINCENT** *exited. Pause. Lights fade on the hut.)*

Scene Three

(Lights rise on **PASTOR** *and* **ANNA** *at table.)*

PASTOR THEO. Give us grateful hearts, our Father, and make us mindful of the needs of others, through Jesus Christ, our Lord. Amen.

ANNA. Amen.

(She rises, starts serving the meal. **VINCENT** *walks in, takes a plate and a butter knife.* **PASTOR THEO** *glares at him.)*

VINCENT. I need it for my painting.

*(***VINCENT** *meets* **PASTOR***'s glare with his own, exits.)*

PASTOR THEO. *(to* **ANNA***)* You will not bring him any food. Do you hear me?

ANNA. But Theodorus –

PASTOR THEO. If he doesn't care to eat with us, fine. But we are not going to indulge him.

ANNA. Yes dear.

PASTOR THEO. Let him eat with the peasants if he likes them so much.

(Lights fade, as the unfinished version of "The Potato Eaters" is again rear-projected on the screen, with the blank swath cutting across the middle, etc.)

(Lights rise on **VINCENT***'s studio at dusk, where he works on a drawing, with the "Potato Eaters" in the background. An unlit candle sits at his elbow.* **VIN** *suddenly reaches for matches, lights the candle, watches the flame. A fantasy* **KAY** *enters, dressed in a nightgown.)*

KAY. I hope I'm not disturbing you…

(She walks over to **VINCENT***, strokes his hair.)*

*(***VINCENT** *tries to ignore her.)*

I just had to tell you: I love you. I love you so deeply. I should have married you and given you a child.

(VINCENT closes his eyes, winces with pain.)

There is nobody else for me, Vincent. I'm still here. I'm still waiting for you. I will always be waiting for you.

VINCENT. No.

KAY. I will never marry anyone else.

VINCENT. *(softly)* I will never marry anyone.

KAY. Save me, Vincent.

VINCENT. I can't.

KAY. I'm drowning here, Vincent. I'm drowning in darkness. Please save me.

VINCENT. *(shaking his head)* Go away.

KAY. Please save me, Vincent. I will die here without you. Save me. Save me. Save me.

VINCENT. Stop it! *(puts his hands over his ears)*

(ANNA VAN GOGH come to the door with a plate of food. ANNA knocks, VINCENT doesn't hear it.)

ANNA. *(knocks again)* Vincent?

(Pause. VINCENT suddenly blows out the candle, turns to ANNA.)

I've brought you some food.

VINCENT. What? Oh… I'm not hungry. *(He returns to working.)*

ANNA. It's just beef stew. Just some carrots and potatoes and beef, the way that you like it…

VINCENT. That's fine, mother. Thank you. Just leave it over there…

ANNA. *(looks around)* Where?

VINCENT. On the table.

ANNA. But there's no room…

VINCENT. *(shoves papers to the side)* There! All right?

ANNA. Don't talk to me like that. You still live in my house. *(puts the plate down)* I hope you won't let it get cold… *(She starts to exit.)* Can I bring you some milk?

VINCENT. No.

ANNA. *(starts to exit again, stops)* Vincent?

VINCENT. Yes mother?

ANNA. It just doesn't seem right… Here we are, living so closely, but we never see you.

VINCENT. Isn't that how you wanted it?

ANNA. No. It's better than yelling and fighting, it's true, but –

VINCENT. Then that's how it should be. Very peaceful.

ANNA. But now that you've been here a while, it just seems that we – that there are other ways for us to –

VINCENT. I don't think so.

ANNA. We're still a family, no matter what's happened… You're part of us and we're part of you, no matter what's been in the past. So couldn't we act as if we weren't such complete enemies?

VINCENT. Why? Does that compromise father too much with the neighbors?

ANNA. I'm not talking about the neighbors now.

VINCENT. No?

ANNA. Will you look at me a moment please?

(VINCENT looks up from his work.)

We've been through a lot, you and I, we're not strangers… You were a wild young boy, a little animal almost, you yelled and howled and threw fits, but you were mine, and I wouldn't let anyone tell me how to raise you –

(VINCENT looks away, bored.)

I am so happy that your work is going well here. I pray every night. But we're not your enemy, do you hear, and I won't have you treating him –

(VIN stops her with a look.)

Do you have any idea what it did to him, losing that hope of advancement, after having to listen to Stricker and the others for years? Do you know what a sacrifice he had to make to let you come back here?

VINCENT. Fine! You're all saints and I am the sinner. You are the martyrs and I am your cross. Now can I get back to work?

ANNA. We love you. Can't you understand that? We love you, and all we want –

VINCENT. No! I would like to leave "love" out of this, please. *(stands, moves away)*

ANNA. Why?

VINCENT. You may not have noticed, but every time that word gets brought up in this household, somebody gets badly hurt... So I'd like to make it a policy from now on to leave that word out of any discussion, or else that discussion will cease...

ANNA. Oh Vincent... I know that's not really you talking...

VINCENT. Believe me, it is.

ANNA. I know how much you've been hurt, and I feel –

VINCENT. Do you, mother?

ANNA. I do. *(pause)*

VINCENT. Look, you were right once before when you called me a savage. I am. So just leave it at that.

ANNA. No...

VINCENT. I wander around the countryside here like a stray dog who's gone back to the wild, and who knows what diseases I have? I may be rabid – watch out. I may be dangerous...

ANNA. Oh, you poor boy... Let me help you.

VINCENT. You can't.

ANNA. Let me try.

VINCENT. No.

*(Pause: **ANNA** puts her arms around **VIN** and holds him.)*

Get away from me.

ANNA. No.

VINCENT. This is not going to work.

ANNA. Just be quiet.

VINCENT. There was a time when... Maybe... But now...

ANNA. We've all hurt each other too much... It's time for forgiveness.

VINCENT. I don't want any more bloodshed...

ANNA. *(still hugging him)* You don't know how long I've wanted to do this... *(She lets go.)* Vincent, will you promise me something?

VINCENT. What?

ANNA. *(holds **VINCENT**'s hand – the one that he burned)* Make peace with your father. Please. He could make trouble for you.

VINCENT. What kind of trouble?

ANNA. Serious trouble.

VINCENT. What do you mean?

ANNA. Just promise me that you'll show him the respect that he needs. Even if you don't feel it.

VINCENT. Will that make you happy, mother?

*(She nods. He shrugs and nods back at her, smiles. **MAGDA** suddenly appears in the doorway, peering in.)*

MAGDA. Vincent? *(She sees **ANNA** and **VINCENT** close together.)* Oh. I'm so sorry. I'll wait out here.

*(**MAGDA** withdraws outside the doorway, Offstage. **ANNA** and **VINCENT** break apart, move away from each other.)*

ANNA. *(sharply)* That's the Hendricke girl, isn't it?

VINCENT. What if it is?

ANNA. She has her nerve, coming here.

VINCENT. I invited her.

ANNA. Did you?

VINCENT. That's right.

ANNA. Well, it doesn't seem wise.

VINCENT. I'll decide that.

ANNA. I've heard some very bad rumors about her... That's not the kind of girl you should be –

VINCENT. *(points to "Potato Eaters")* I'm using her for my painting.

ANNA. That doesn't change how it looks –

VINCENT. Please go now.

ANNA. There's your father's reputation to consider. You can't be so reckless –

*(**VINCENT** flips the plate off the table, shattering the dish, spilling the stew.)*

VINCENT. I have my work to do. All right? I can't help who I am.

ANNA. Don't forget you're also his son.

VINCENT. How could I? *(pause)*

ANNA. *(looks down at broken dish)* I'll clean this up.

VINCENT. I'll take care of it.

ANNA. *(down on her knees)* I'm not going to have that girl see this. *(She starts picking up pieces.)*

VINCENT. Mother…

*(He forcibly raises **ANNA** up off the floor.)*

ANNA. *(still resisting)* No –

VINCENT. I will do it. *(Pause. Then he calls out:)* Magda!

MAGDA. *(enters)* Yes sir?

*(**ANNA** turns around and heads for the door. **ANNA** stops for a moment to glare at **MAGDA**. Then **ANNA** exits.)*

I'm sorry, but I didn't know where else to look for you, and it's very important –

VINCENT. It's just as well that you've come.

MAGDA. What?

VINCENT. I have a problem that I haven't been able to solve, and – *(He takes her hand.)* Come over here…

(He brings her around to the side of his table, stepping over dish.)

MAGDA. *(looks down at the spilled stew)* But – I have to tell you –

VINCENT. Yous remember that painting I told you about – of the family at supper?

MAGDA. Yes sir, I do. But –

VINCENT. *(points to unfinished canvas)* Well, I've pretty much worked out the positions, but there's this fifth person – she keeps coming back into the picture, no matter how many times I take her out…and I just can't figure out where she belongs.

MAGDA. I'm sure this is very important, but there's something I –

VINCENT. Now the logical place for her is right here, at the head of the table… That only makes sense, don't you think? If she's serving the food…

*(***VINCENT*** positions ***MAGDA*** like this, facing the audience.)*

But the thing is – I haven't been able to *see* her expression, no matter how many times I've tried…

MAGDA. Herr Vincent please, just let me –

VINCENT. Do you think you could do that for me? Just imagine yourself at this meal, the shack is filled with the smell of roasted potatoes, and you reach down into a large bowl with a big wooden spoon, the heat and smoke rising up into your face, and you –

MAGDA. You shouldn't have said those things to me the other day.

VINCENT. What?

MAGDA. You said some very mean things.

VINCENT. Did I?

MAGDA. Yes.

VINCENT. Well, it happens sometimes, you shouldn't take it personally. Now if we could…

MAGDA. It's all because of you that these other things happened.

VINCENT. What other things?

MAGDA. *(bursts into tears)* Oh Vincent…

(*She runs into his arms, putting her head on his chest.*)

VINCENT. What's wrong? *(pause)*

MAGDA. I'm pregnant.

VINCENT. I'm not sure I understand… Is the father unwilling to marry you?

MAGDA. Yes.

VINCENT. Would you like me to speak with him for you?

MAGDA. No.

VINCENT. Shall I speak with your mother?

MAGDA. No! I mean…thank you, Vincent, but… Why couldn't you have just gone with me? What would it have hurt? I would never have told a soul!

VINCENT. What have you done, Magda?

MAGDA. Oh Vincent… I told them…

VINCENT. Yes?

MAGDA. I said it was yours.

VINCENT. Why would you do that?

MAGDA. Because you yelled at me.

VINCENT. What?

MAGDA. You said some very bad things.

VINCENT. And they believed you?

MAGDA. Oh yes. Everyone thinks you're my lover.

VINCENT. What do you mean by "everyone"?

MAGDA. Everyone in the village, of course.

VINCENT. You mean, more than your mother knows?

MAGDA. Everyone in the village thinks you're the father. Even the real father does.

VINCENT. Then you must tell everyone that you lied.

MAGDA. Oh, they would never believe me. They'd think I was protecting you.

VINCENT. Nonsense.

MAGDA. It's true.

(**VINCENT** *walks away, thinking.*)

Oh Vincent, I'm sorry! I'm so very sorry! *(pause)* Aren't you angry with me?

(**VINCENT** *struggles, trying not to lash out at her.*)

VINCENT. You'll have to leave now.

MAGDA. But Herr Vincent!

VINCENT. I'm busy... I'll try to take care of this later... We'll see if we can straighten it out. *(takes out his sketchpad, sits)*

MAGDA. But a group of them have gone to the Pastor today! That's what I came here to tell you... They are talking to the Pastor right now. *(pause)*

VINCENT. *(stops working)* Are you sure?

MAGDA. Yes. Would you like me to talk with him for you?

VINCENT. *(stands, grabs her hand)* You're going to tell them what a liar you are.

MAGDA. *(thrilled)* Oh, I will, Vincent! I will! I'll tell them how we were all alone, and I tried to show you Mama's soft bed, but you wouldn't –

(**VINCENT** *flicks her hand away from him.*)

I swear to you, I'll tell everything – how many men have seen Mama's bed, and that even if you had gone with me, I could never be sure it was –

VINCENT. Oh God...

MAGDA. I am terribly sorry.

VINCENT. How will I ever finish...finish this...?

(**VINCENT** *suddenly grabs her by the shoulders, shakes her, brings his arm back to slap her...then drops his hand, turning away.*)

MAGDA. I really didn't mean for this to happen, Herr Vincent.

VINCENT. Leave, Magda.

MAGDA. You have to believe me.

VINCENT. Just go away.

MAGDA. I'll pray for you, Vincent. I will.

(There is a slight smile on her face as she exits.)

VINCENT. How could this happen? How could this ever happen? *(looks back at the painting for a long beat)* I will find you, whatever happens… I have not come all this way, just to leave your face blank. I will figure you out. I will paint you.

*(**VINCENT** walks out of the studio, as the lights fade.)*

Scene Four

(Lights rise on **PASTOR THEO** *at his desk, writing in a large book.* **ANNA** *enters.)*

ANNA. Theodorus?

PASTOR THEO. *(without looking up)* Yes?

ANNA. I would like to be present too.

PASTOR THEO. No.

ANNA. He's my son as well. *(pause)* There's something I suppose I should tell you...

PASTOR THEO. Yes?

ANNA. I saw him with this girl today. She came to his studio while I was there. But I've also heard that other men in the village have –

PASTOR THEO. I don't care about other men.

ANNA. But don't you see? It means that Vincent may not be the –

PASTOR THEO. Send him in please.

ANNA. Theodorus...

PASTOR THEO. Right now.

ANNA. Theodorus.

PASTOR THEO. Did you hear me?

ANNA. Please promise me that you will not mention that other thing. That terrible

PASTOR THEO. *(stands)* Anna.

ANNA. Promise me.

PASTOR THEO. I will not.

ANNA. Promise me, or I will leave you.

PASTOR THEO. How dare you.

ANNA. I will leave this house and never see you again.

PASTOR THEO. Do you know what you're saying?

ANNA. Yes.

PASTOR THEO. You are willing to put our own marriage at risk? *(pause)* Anna... I'm astonished at your behavior.

*(**ANNA** is unflinching. Finally, the **PASTOR** nods. **ANNA** leaves the room. **VINCENT** enters.)*

PASTOR THEO. Close the door. *(**VIN** closes the door.)* Sit down.

VINCENT. If it's all the same to you, father –

PASTOR THEO. Sit down.

*(Pause: **VINCENT** sits.)*

VINCENT. Before we start in with this –

PASTOR THEO. No one gave you permission to speak.

VINCENT. I would just like to try to avoid any –

*(**PASTOR** looks up: pause.)*

PASTOR THEO. A short time ago, I received a visit from the village elders.

VINCENT. I know.

PASTOR THEO. Do you?

VINCENT. Yes, and I want to –

PASTOR THEO. It seems there's been a wolf invading my flock…and that wolf is my son.

VINCENT. If you're referring to the woman Magda –

PASTOR THEO. You know very well what I'm referring to.

VINCENT. Don't take this tone with me, father, or we will both regret it. *(pause)* You may think you know the whole truth here…

PASTOR THEO. You've gone too far this time, boy. I've used my influence to save you before, but –

VINCENT. Please listen to what I have to say before you condemn me.

PASTOR THEO. Go ahead.

VINCENT. I swear to you, father, this woman and I have never been intimate. Never. I swear on my soul. *(pause)* She posed for me, yes – but that's it. I don't know where she came up with her story.

PASTOR THEO. What story is that?

VINCENT. That I fathered her child.

PASTOR THEO. So you know that she's pregnant?

VINCENT. She told me.

PASTOR THEO. So you're still seeing her?

VINCENT. No. I mean…

PASTOR THEO. You mean that you've seen her more than just once?

VINCENT. But only to –

PASTOR THEO. *(shakes his head)* Vincent.

VINCENT. I swear to you, father –

PASTOR THEO. No! Don't swear anymore. Don't put yourself in deeper peril.

VINCENT. But you have to understand –

PASTOR THEO. Oh, I understand perfectly.

VINCENT. Believe me, you don't.

PASTOR THEO. I happen to know that you saw her today, even while I was trying to defend you.

VINCENT. I never said I hadn't seen her, but it was only to –

PASTOR THEO. No! You've had your say, now I'm going to have mine. *(pause)* I see no other recourse than for you to marry her.

VINCENT. *(stands)* What?

PASTOR THEO. You heard me.

VINCENT. But the woman means nothing to me.

PASTOR THEO. You should have thought of that before –

VINCENT. I already told you! I never –

PASTOR THEO. And I don't believe you.

VINCENT. I am not marrying her.

PASTOR THEO. Oh, but you are.

VINCENT. I'm telling you, father –

PASTOR THEO. *(looks down at his work)* You can go now. We will talk about the arrangements tomorrow. It will be a quiet country wedding, the sort peasants enjoy…

VINCENT. You pious bastard…

PASTOR THEO. *(not looking up)* Please shut the door when you leave.

VINCENT. Who do you think you are?

PASTOR THEO. *(sharply)* What?

VINCENT. You think you're God, telling me what to do?

PASTOR THEO. I know just who I am. I am Theodorus van Gogh, pastor of a small country town. And who are you?

VINCENT. Your son.

PASTOR THEO. Then please act like it for once.

(**PASTOR** *looks down.* **VINCENT** *knocks the book off his desk.*)

If you leave now, I will try to disregard that. Otherwise…

VINCENT. Yes?

PASTOR THEO. I will have to ask you to remove yourself from these grounds. *(pause)* I threw you out of this house once before, I can do it again.

VINCENT. *(turns away)* You're making a bad mistake, father…

PASTOR THEO. And don't think that Theo will come to your aid this time.

VINCENT. Oh no?

PASTOR THEO. You will die all alone in a ditch, like a dog in its vomit.

(pause)

VINCENT. It so happens, father, that someone else has offered me shelter.

PASTOR THEO. Who? Your new whore?

VINCENT. No. The sexton of the Catholic church.

PASTOR THEO. What?

VINCENT. That's right. He's been kind enough to offer me a room behind the Chapel.

PASTOR THEO. I don't believe you.

VINCENT. Then don't.

PASTOR THEO. I forbid you… He's just using you to get at me. He's been trying for years.

VINCENT. So have I. *(pause)*

PASTOR THEO. Do you have any idea how that would... It would make me a laughingstock –

(VINCENT turns to leave.)

I forbid you!

(As VINCENT walks away, PASTOR grabs him by the shoulder, holding him back. VINCENT pulls away, PASTOR falls back.)

VINCENT. What happened to you, father? What happened? You were so gentle, so caring – I worshipped you growing up.

PASTOR THEO. *(turns away)* Vincent...

VINCENT. I remember how you used to get up in the middle of the night and go off if anyone needed you... You were strong then, because you *believed*. You didn't care what anyone thought.

PASTOR THEO. Oh, I still believe. I see God in his tower demanding obedience, and those who don't give it must suffer.

VINCENT. The God you taught me to love saw people's weaknesses and forgave them...

PASTOR THEO. That's a convenient idea for you, isn't it?

VINCENT. It was *your* idea.

PASTOR THEO. If there's one thing I've learned in this lifetime, it is that God doesn't come when we call. And why should He? *(pause)*

VINCENT. I feel very sad for you, father.

PASTOR THEO. Well, I'm not the one who's in trouble here.

VINCENT. Aren't you?

PASTOR THEO. This is deeper than you may think, boy. If you move in with the sexton, I will take action.

VINCENT. What do you mean?

PASTOR THEO. There's a place I've looked into at Zundert. A sanitarium.

VINCENT. What?

PASTOR THEO. That's right, boy. An asylum. It is not pleasant, but it is efficient.

VINCENT. Father… I'm not a child. You can't just put me away.

PASTOR THEO. I will if I have to.

VINCENT. You have no grounds.

PASTOR THEO. Don't I? You smear yourself all over with coaldust, you propose to your own cousin, you stick your hand in a fire, and now –

VINCENT. That's enough.

PASTOR THEO. I'll say it is.

VINCENT. *(nervously rubbing his chin)* Is mother a part of this too?

PASTOR THEO. Part of what?

VINCENT. Part of this plan to dispose of me.

PASTOR THEO. There is no plan.

VINCENT. Oh no?

PASTOR THEO. But your mother is aware of everything that goes on in this household.

VINCENT. I don't believe it.

PASTOR THEO. How could it be otherwise?

*(**VINCENT** starts pacing around the room in a panic.)*

Now this is just what I'm talking about! Show some self-control!

VINCENT. *(pacing)* I'll never finish it.

PASTOR THEO. What?

VINCENT. *(sits in the chair, his head in his hands)* I'll never finish the painting.

PASTOR THEO. Oh, I'm sure they'll let you continue your work there. Maybe not for the first six months or so…

VINCENT. Six months!

PASTOR THEO. Or maybe a year, I don't know. They have their own methods of treatment. Their rules. You will have to respect them.

(**VINCENT** *shakes his head, defeated.*)

I wish there was some other way, boy…

VINCENT. But there is… *(approaches)* Why can't you just believe in me, trust me?

PASTOR THEO. I'm afraid it's not as simple as that.

VINCENT. Why can't you simply love me as your own son?

PASTOR THEO. *(turns away)* It's too late for that.

VINCENT. No.

(*He puts his arms around the* **PASTOR***, embraces him.*)

PASTOR THEO. *(trying to squirm away)* Don't – Vincent, you mustn't –

VINCENT. *(holds on)* We can't give in to that hatred. We can't act as if there's no hope.

PASTOR THEO. *(struggling)* Vincent, no! Let me go!

(*There is a flash of light upstage right, then the projection of "The Potato Eaters" appears, with a live figure juxtaposed, her back to both* **VINCENT** *and the audience, in the position she occupies in the finished version.*)

VINCENT. I see her now, father.

PASTOR THEO. Vincent! Listen to me!

VINCENT. I see her.

PASTOR THEO. Stop this!

VINCENT. She's a young girl at the start of her life who has made her first dinner.

PASTOR THEO. I demand that you stop this!

VINCENT. We don't have to see her face! We can just feel her spirit!

(*The figure takes off her peasant's cap, turns around: it is* **KAY***. She looks at* **VINCENT***, who squeezes* **PASTOR***.*)

PASTOR THEO. I demand – ! I demand – !

(ANNA opens door.)

ANNA. Is everything all right?

(Upstage right scene goes black: KAY exits, the projection vanishes.)

I thought I heard shouting –

PASTOR THEO. *(weakly)* Anna.

(VINCENT lets go. PASTOR totters, falls to one knee.)

ANNA. Theodorus!

PASTOR THEO. *(gasping)* I'll be all right in one…in one…

VINCENT. *(approaches PASTOR, bends down)* I love you, father.

(VINCENT kisses PASTOR on the forehead, then walks swiftly out. ANNA loosens PASTOR's collar, etc., as the lights dim on the study.)

Scene Five

(Church bells start tolling. **REVEREND PETERSON** *enters, holding a large black umbrella over his head. parish women enter, also holding umbrellas.* **ANNA** *and* **PASTOR THEO** *exit. The tolling stops.)*

REV. PETERSON. We are gathered here for the funeral of a great man. Not just a great man of the cloth, but a great man of the heart. He loved his parishioners like family, and he loved his family like no one else I've ever known...

*(***REVEREND PETERSON*** *and the parish women exit.* **VINCENT** *and* **THEO** *enter the clearing with the acacia tree, dressed in dark mourning clothes.)*

VINCENT. Say it.

THEO. No.

VINCENT. Say it! *(pause)* I killed him, Theo.

THEO. No.

VINCENT. I killed him.

THEO. You didn't... I'm the one who said to come back here. It's on my head.

VINCENT. No.

THEO. It's on my head too.

VINCENT. I absolve you, brother.

THEO. You can't.

VINCENT. I absolve you.

THEO. You bastard! You think that's going to help me?

VINCENT. Help you?

THEO. Yes. Help me. *(pause)* He had his flaws, but he loved you. He loved you deeply.

VINCENT. Did he?

THEO. And now he's gone. We have no home.

VINCENT. We'll make a new one.

THEO. Mother will have to go live with the Strickers. She'll never have her own place again. There will never be a place for us to come back to.

VINCENT. You can always think of us here, by our tree, speaking truth to each other.

THEO. This clearing is gone.

VINCENT. No.

THEO. It's gone… We'll never come back here again.

VINCENT. I will always be here in this clearing with you.

*(***THEO*** *shakes his head.)*

I will always be here in this clearing with you.

*(***THEO*** *listens.)*

I will always be here in this clearing with you.

*(***THEO***, looking downstage towards audience, extends his Upstage arm towards* **VINCENT**. **VINCENT** *extends his arm toward* **THEO**. *The Lights fade slowly to black.)*

End of Play

PROPERTY PLOT

Wheelbarrow
China tea service
Plates and serving trays
Sketchpad and pencils
Artist's palette and easel
Stationery and pens
Gardening tools
Potatoes
Knife
Bucket
Candelabra and candle